Garage Band

Garage Band

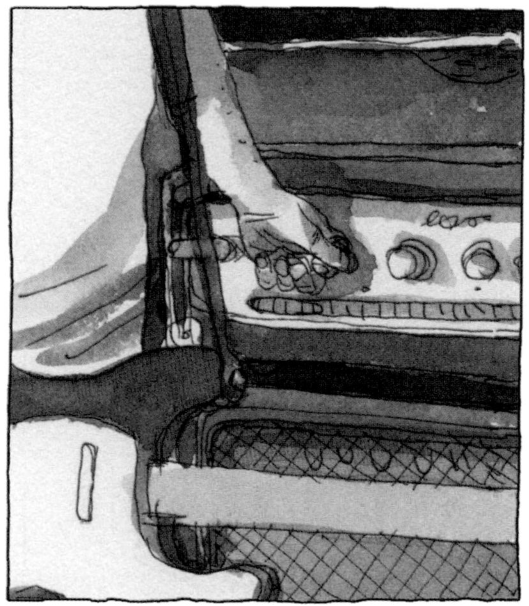

Gipi

TRANSLATION BY
SPECTRUM

Prima Canzone

THIS IS IT...

THIS IS THE PLACE.

NO WORK

WOOF WOOF WOOF

IT´S JUST TEMPORARY - A GIFT FROM MY DAD.

AND WHAT´RE WE SUPPOSED TO DO WITH IT?

SNIFF

CLEAR IT OUT, CLEAN IT UP, GET THE PLACE WIRED UP -

WOOF

WOOF

WOOF

AND THEN BRING IN THE INSTRUMENTS.

THE ROOM´S MINE AS LONG AS I STAY OUT OF TROUBLE.

THAT´S THE RULE FOR THE TEMPORARY GIFT.

OK.
BAM

THIS PLACE IS FULL OF RAT CRAP.
WE'RE GONNA GET LEPTOSPIROSIS FOR SURE. TWENTY-FOUR HOURS OF EXCRUCIATING PAIN.
AND THEN WE'LL GO INTO SPASMS AND CROAK.

YOU THINK SO?
SCRATCH

THERE'S NO CURE FOR IT.

I THINK IT'LL LOOK GREAT IF WE CLEAN IT UP.
SNIFF

WOOF
WOOF
WOOF
WOOF
WOOF
WOOF

WOOF
WOOF
WOOF
WOOF
WOOF
WOOF
WOOF
WOOF
WOOF
WOOF

WOOF
WOOF
WOOF
WOOF
WOOF

AND THOSE DOGS?
THEY'RE MY DAD'S DOGS.

AND WHEN WE RECORD? ARE WE GONNA RECORD THE DOGS TOO?
"LIVE AT THE DOG POUND"?
WOOF
WOOF
WOOF
WOOF
WOOF
WOOF
WOOF

THEY'RE TRAINED DOGS. WE'LL KEEP THEM QUIET.
THEY'RE REALLY SMART.
YEAH, SURE, WE'LL JUST TALK TO THEM.
WOOF WOOF WOOF

WOOF WOOF PLEASE
BE QUIET WOOF WOOF

YIP YIP YIP

MY DAD'S DOGS ARE CHAMPION HUNTERS AND SHOW DOGS.
MY DAD HUNTS HARE, PHEASANT, WOODCOCK, SNIPE, AND BLACKBIRD.

I'M ALWAYS FINDING DEAD PHEASANTS IN THE FRIDGE AT HOME.
THESE BIRDS HAVE BEAUTIFUL FEATHERS.
FLAP
FLAP
FLAP
WOOF
WOOF
WOOF

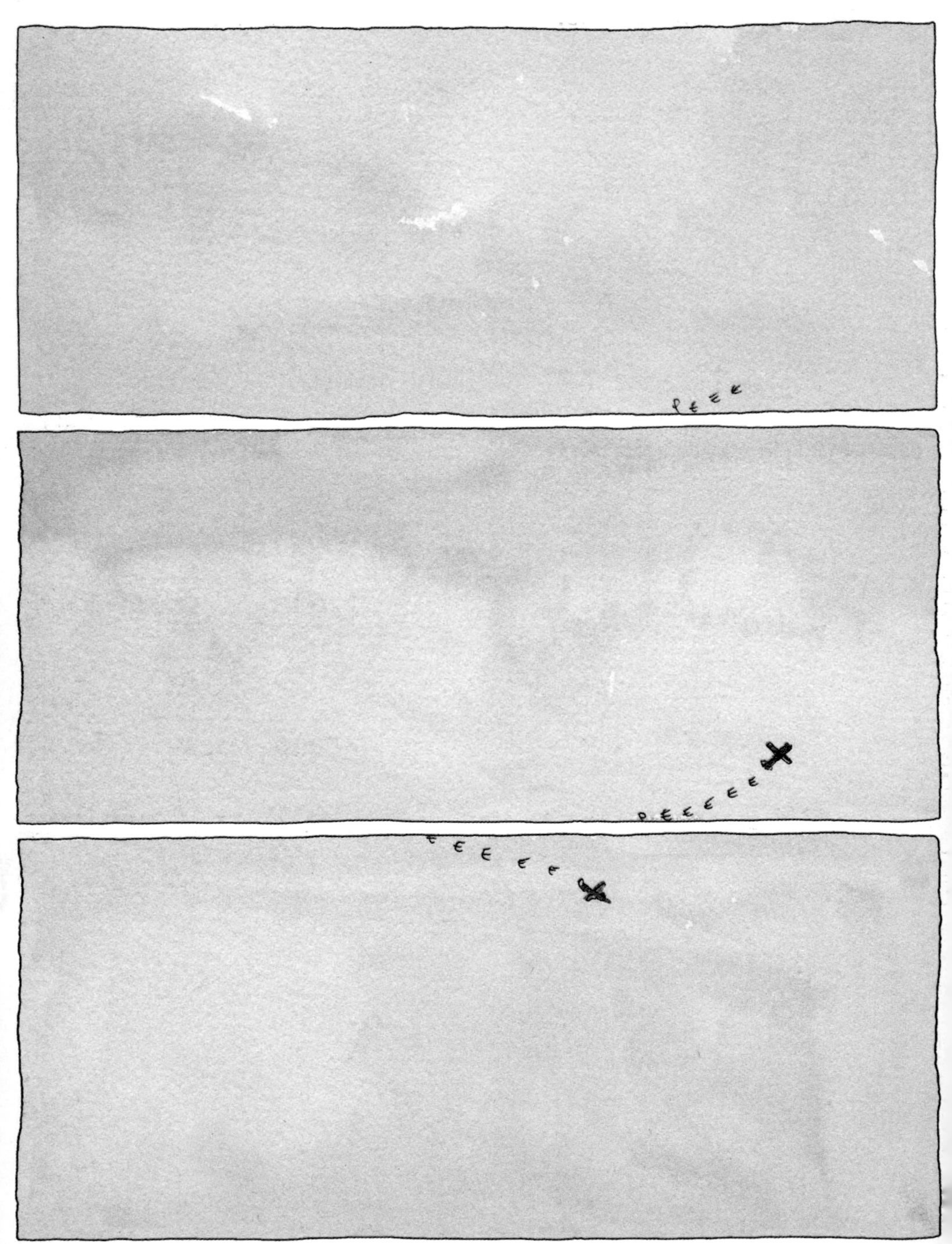

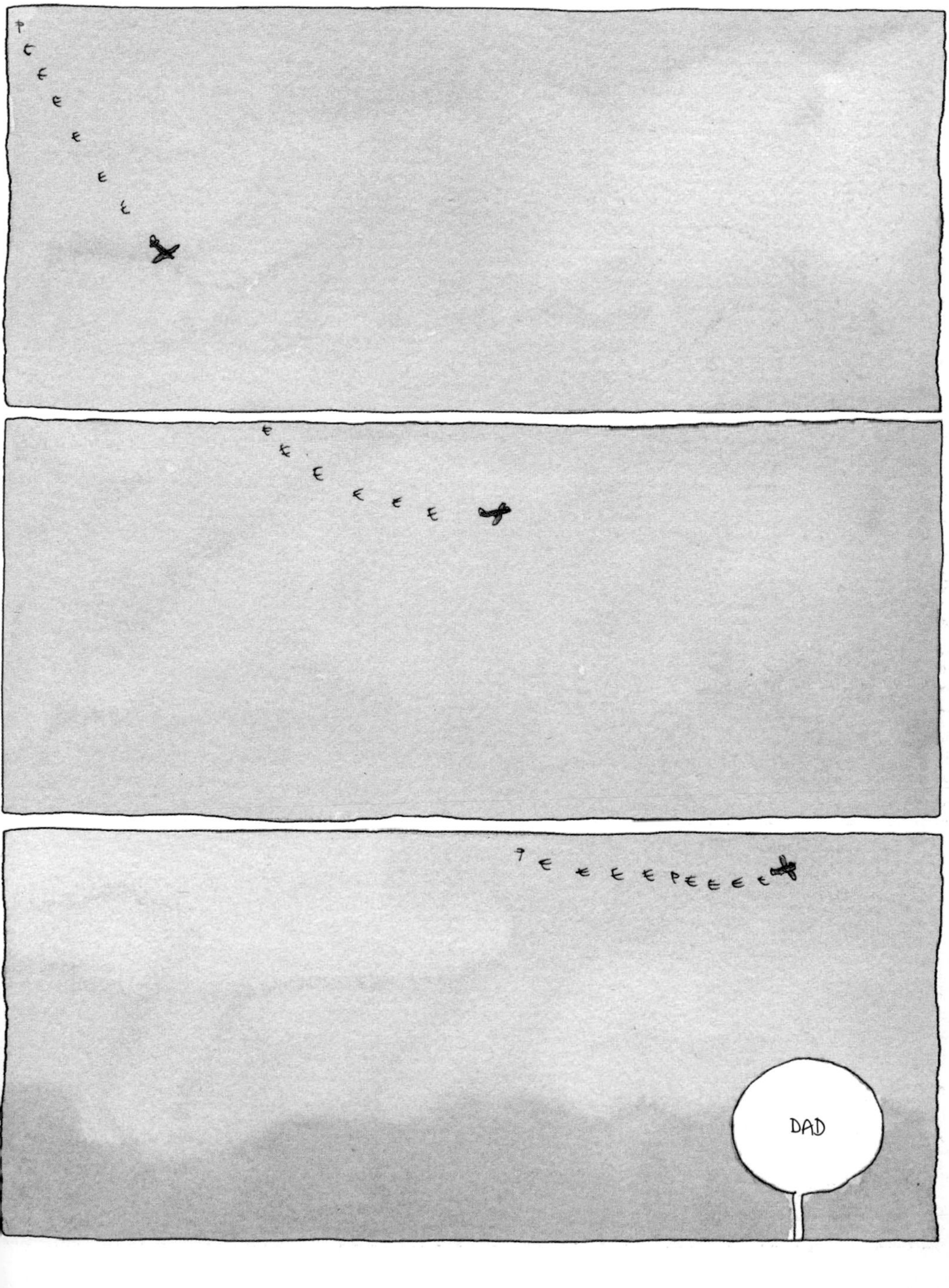

PEEEEEE

EEEEEE

PEEEEPEEEEE

DAD

WATCH THIS DIVE.
PEEE
DAD, I NEED THE CAR.
EEEEEE
I'VE GOT TO TAKE THE INSTRUMENTS TO THE GARAGE.
EEEEEEEE
PEEE
YOU'LL HAVE TO ASK YOUR MOM.
EEEE
MY WORD DOESN'T COUNT FOR MUCH ANY MORE.
PEEEEEEEE
SHE TOLD ME TO ASK YOU.
SHE SAYS YOU'RE STILL THE BOSS.

YEAH, I WISH...

I'M THE PILOT.

BUT SHE'S THE CAPTAIN NOW.
PHUT PHUT

PHUT PHUT PHUT PHUT

TAKE THE WINGS OFF FIRST.

KER-CLICK

I HAVE TO TAKE THE BASS AND THE AMP OVER TO THE GARAGE.
I CAN'T DO IT WITH THE BIKE. I TOTALLY NEED THE CAR.

Ein Volk
ein Reich
ein Führer
EDIZIONI "LA STORIA IMMORTALE" - © 2005 - PRINTED IN ITALY

SHLUP

FRRR
WOW, WHAT A FIND...

100 EUROS WELL SPENT.
KNOCK KNOCK KNOCK
ALEX

YEAH?
ALEX, WE'RE READY.

ALL RIGHT.
PUT EVERYTHING IN THE CAR, I'LL BE RIGHT DOWN.

SO WHO DOES THIS GARAGE BELONG TO?
BRRRMMM

RAT-A-TAT
RAT-A-TAT
RRM
WHO'LL BE THERE?

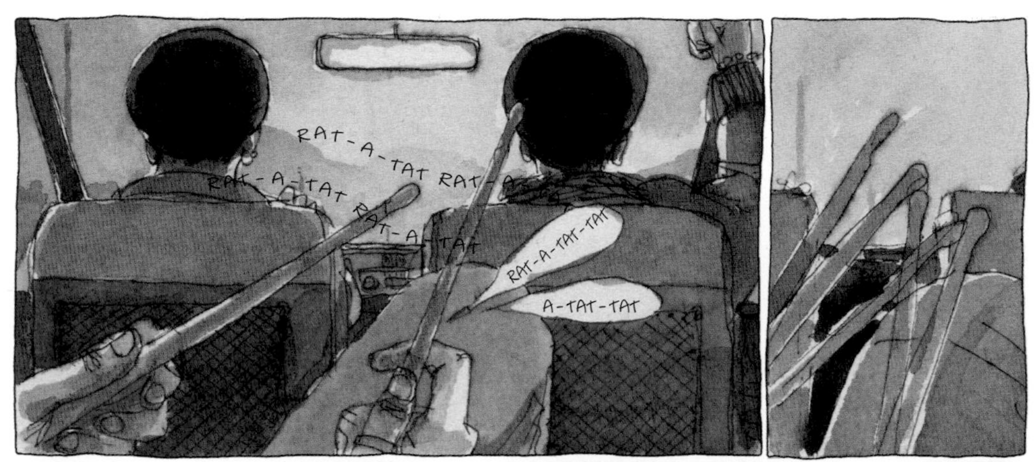
RAT-A-TAT RAT-A-TAT
RAT-A-TAT
RAT-A-TAT
RAT-A-TAT-TAT
A-TAT-TAT

I HOPE THERE WON'T BE ANY TROUBLEMAKERS THERE.
NO.
WHOOSH
BRRRRMMM
RAT-A-TAT
RAT-A
RAT-A-TAT
RAT-A-TAT-TAT
RAT-A-TAT-TAT

WHOOSH
BRRRRMMM
RAT-A-TAT
RAT-A-TAT-TAT

THAT CRAZY KID YOU WENT TO SCHOOL WITH WON'T BE THERE, WILL HE?
OH NO, AUNT, HE DEFINITELY WON'T BE THERE.

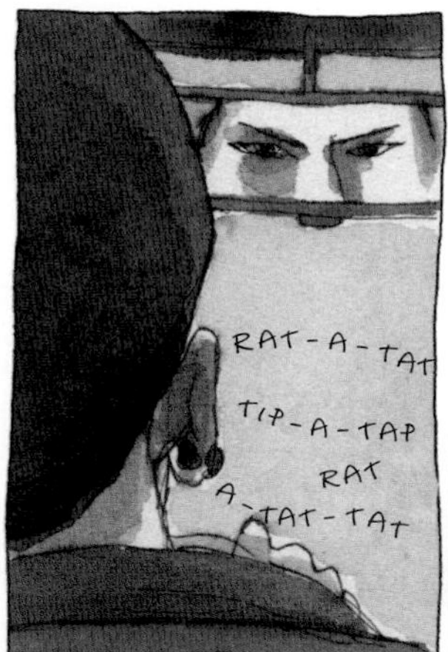
RAT-A-TAT
TIP-A-TAP
RAT
A-TAT-TAT

RAT-A-TAT
TIP-A-TAP
SO, WHO'S PAYING FOR THIS DARNED GARAGE FOR YOU?
BRRRRRMM

IT BELONGS TO GIULIANO'S DAD.
WE'RE NOT PAYING A CENT.

LUCKY HIM, BEING A GENTLEMAN HE CAN AFFORD TO GIVE PRESENTS.
BRRRRMM

BRRRM
IT'S EASY TO BE GENEROUS IF YOU HAVE THAT MUCH MONEY.
HOW TRUE!

LOOK AT THIS, GIULIANO.
THE WHITE MAN WITH HIS NATIVE PORTERS.
HE'S A GENIUS.

PANT PANT
HE'S A DRUMMER. HE CAN'T BE A GENIUS.

DRUMMING RESULTS IN THE ONGOING, IRREVERSIBLE DEVELOPMENT OF MICROLESIONS IN THE BRAIN.

STEFANO!

STEFANO, HIDE! DON'T LET THEM SEE YOU!

AND WHY, MIGHT I ASK?
YOU KNOW WHY.
DON'T GET ME INTO TROUBLE.

ALEX!
COME ON, HIDE, PLEASE!
I EXIST - YOU HUMANS CANNOT CONTINUE TO DENY IT!

OOF

GIULIANO, WHAT DOES YOUR DAD DO? IS HE A DOCTOR?
RUSTLE RUSTLE RUSTLE
OR A VETERINARIAN? WHAT'S HE DO? THERE'S A BUNCH OF WICKED COOL STUFF HERE...

HEY, STEFANO, BE QUIET!
STAY HIDDEN. DON'T LET THEM SEE YOU.

ALEX, YOU'VE GOT TWO MINUTES TO CHASE OFF THE OLD FOGIES. THEN I'M COMING OUT AND GIVING 'EM A HEART ATTACK.
YOU HAVE TWO MINUTES, STARTING RIGHT NOW.

ALEX!
YEAH, MOM...
ALEX, HUH HUH
BAM

WOOF
WOOF

JUST PUT EVERYTHING HERE AND GO AWAY.
WE'LL DEAL WITH EVERYTHING, YOU CAN GO NOW. JUST GO.
HELLO, MA'AM. HOW ARE YOU?

WOOF WOOF
OH...
GOOD HEAVENS, GIULIANO, YOU'VE LOST SO MUCH WEIGHT!

AW, YOU'RE JOKING, I STILL WEIGH JUST THE SAME...
130 POUNDS EXACTLY.

I SUPPOSE YOU'RE RIGHT.
WELL, LOOK AT WHAT DADDY'S GIVEN YOU!
WOOF
WOOF

HE'S ONLY LENDING IT TO ME. IT'S NOT A REAL PRESENT.

WELL, IT'S NICE TO BE GENEROUS IF YOU CAN AFFORD IT!
MOM, THAT'S ENOUGH, YOU CAN GO NOW.
IT'S HOT IN HERE, YOU'LL GET SICK, AND IT'S LATE.

WOOF
WOOF
WOOF
NO RUSH, EH?

IT'S FOR YOUR OWN GOOD.

WOOF
WOOF
WOOF
WOOF
WOOF
WOOF

WOOF
WOOF
WOOF
WOOF

WON'T ALL THAT BARKING GET ON YOUR NERVES?
WOOF
WOOF
WOOF

THEY'RE MY DAD'S DOGS, THEY'RE ALL CHAMPION HUNTERS AND SHOW DOGS.
WOOF
WOOF
WOOF
DON'T WORRY ABOUT THE DOGS, MA'AM.
RUSTLE

I HAVE BEEN SENT BY THE DEPARTMENT OF PUBLIC HEALTH TO EXTERMINATE THEM BY MEANS OF LETHAL INJECTION.

THANKS TO THIS LITTLE DISCOVERY...

THE ANIMAL WILL BE SEIZED WITH PAINFUL AND UNCONTROLLABLE CONVULSIONS.
ARF...

ARGH...

THE TONGUE SWELLS UP AND BECOMES LIKE SANDPAPER.
AND THE BLOOD STARTS TO BOIL, COOKING THE INTERNAL ORGANS.

GLURGH...

AND FINALLY, THE ANIMAL DIES.
SUFFOCATED BY ITS OWN VOMIT.

YOU CAN STAY AND WATCH IF YOU WANT.

CLAP CLAP

NICE JOB.
THAT WAS SMART.
CLAP CLAP

NOW, DO YOU HAVE EVEN THE SLIGHTEST IDEA OF THE MESS YOU'VE GOT ME INTO?
ALEX!

BRRM

DUM DA DUM
DUM DA DUM
DUM DA DUM
TUM TUM

DUM DA DUM
DUM DUM

COME ON, MOM, ARE YOU KIDDING?

IT WASN'T HIM. THAT WAS A REAL VET. IT'S GOT NOTHING TO DO WITH ME.
I DIDN'T KNOW ANYTHING ABOUT THE DOGS, DID I?
BRRRRMMM
THE AUTHORITIES MUST HAVE SENT FOR HIM. I'M TELLING THE TRUTH.

HERE´S ALBERTO.
BRRMMM

ALBERTO-COME-LATELY.

HEY
I SAW THAT FOOL OUTSIDE WITH HIS MOTHER AND AUNT LOOKING REALLY PISSED OFF.
WHAT HAVE YOU BEEN UP TO?

AND YOU?
I WAS AT MY DAD´S.

YOU MISSED A GREAT SHOW.
I´LL TAKE THE AMP.

YOU´VE GOTTA BE ON TIME WHEN WE´RE PRACTICING.
CLICK
YOU WANNA BE A NURSE OR A MUSICIAN? YOU´VE GOTTA MAKE UP YOUR MIND.

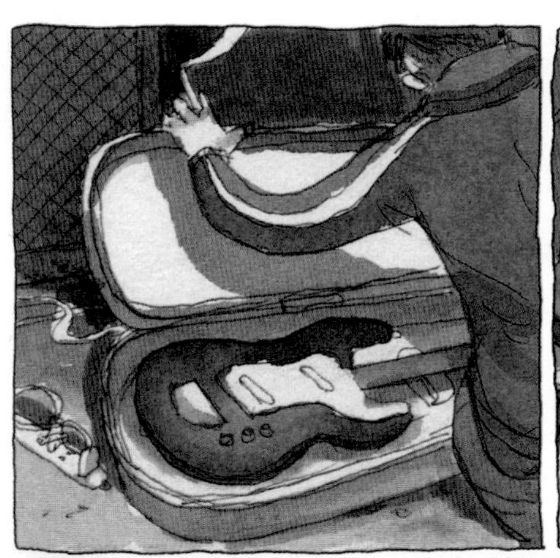

ALBERTO'S FATHER WAS ALWAYS HEALTHY.
SELEN
HE WAS SICK ONLY ONCE.
TUM TUM

BUT THAT WAS ENOUGH TO TURN HIM INTO A DIFFERENT PERSON.

BLANG BLANG

TAC TAC
THIS FIRST SONG IS ALSO ABOUT HIM.

AND IT'S ABOUT ALEX, WITH HIS STUPID NAZI FANTASIES.

ABOUT HIS MOTHER AND HIS AUNT.
AND THE AFTERNOON THEY WILL SPEND IN THEIR PARKED CAR, SPYING ON ALEX AND HIS FRIENDS.

AND FINALLY, IT'S ABOUT THE GARAGE ITSELF.
ABOUT HOW GLAD WE ARE TO HAVE A PLACE TO PRACTICE.
A PLACE ALL OUR OWN.

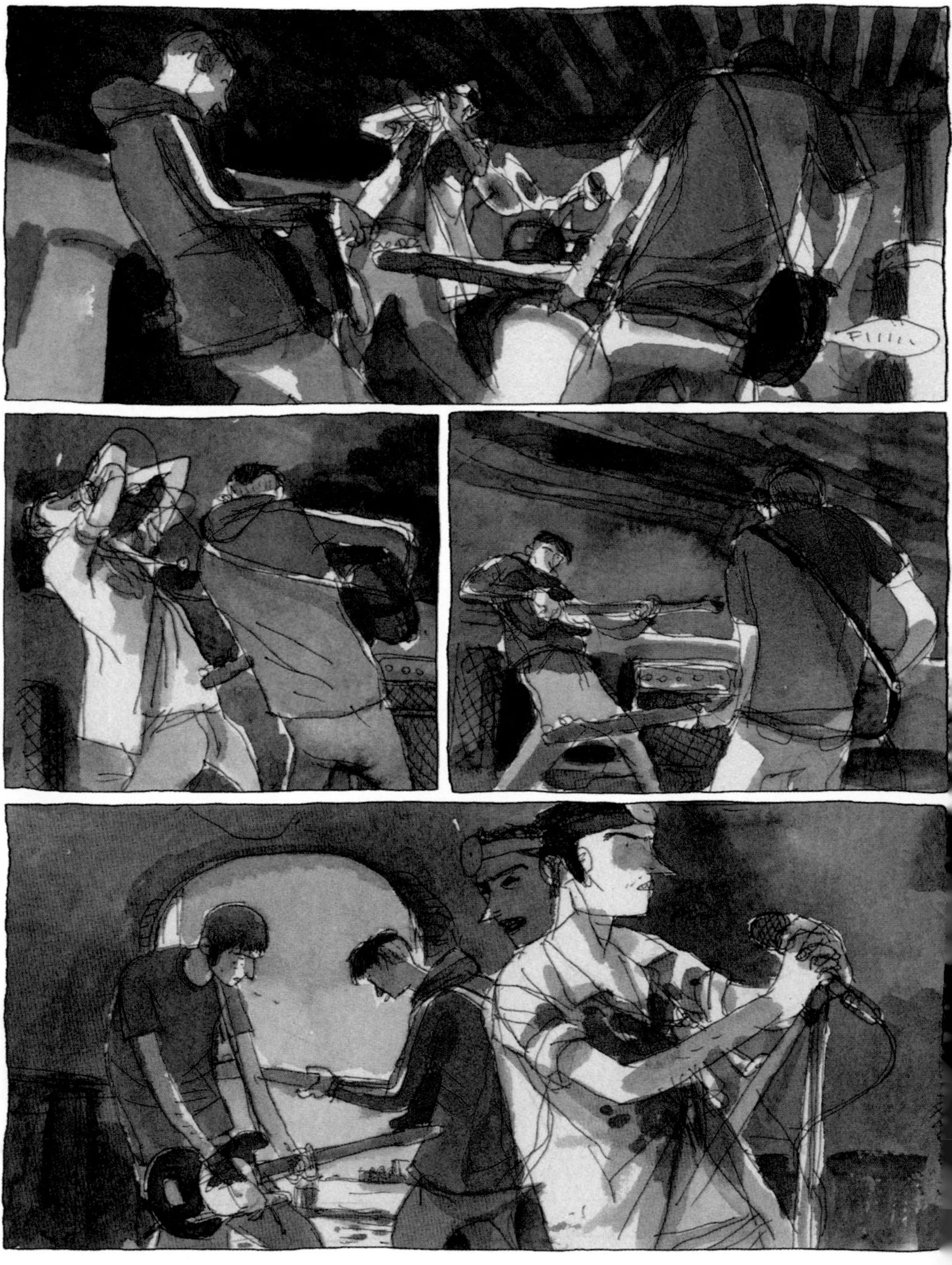

FIIIII

Seconda Canzone

AND THEN WHAT'RE YOU GONNA DO?

I DON'T KNOW.
WE'LL GET SOME SONGS READY, AND THEN WE'LL SEE. EVERYTHING'S DIFFERENT NOW WE'VE GOT THE GARAGE.

HAVING OUR OWN PLACE TO PRACTICE IN IS THE BEST THING IN THE WORLD.

BOOOOOMMM

SO, TELL ME SOME-THING
HAVE YOU STILL GOT THAT NAZI GUY ON THE DRUMS?

YEAH, BUT HE'S NOT A REAL NAZI.
HE'S AN IDIOT MORE THAN ANYTHING ELSE.

MAYBE ...
BUT I COULDN'T SPEND TIME WITH SOMEONE WHO HAD A POSTER OF HITLER ON HIS BEDROOM WALL.
ME NEITHER, IF I THOUGHT IT WAS FOR REAL.

HE'S JUST AN IDIOT.
HE'S JUST FAS-CINATED BY THE AESTHETIC. HE DOESN'T KNOW A THING ABOUT NAZISM.
BOOOOOMMM

HE LIKES THE UNIFORMS, THE LEATHER TRENCHCOATS, THE INSIGNIA.
IN SHORT, HE'S AN IDIOT.
SCRATCH
ANYONE WOULD THINK THAT "IDIOT" WAS A COMPLIMENT, COMING FROM YOU.

I DON'T KNOW.
BUT BETTER AN IDIOT THAN A NAZI, DON'T YOU THINK?

DOES HE PLAY WELL, AT LEAST?

YEAH. HE'S GOOD.
BUT HE'S A DRUMMER. STEFANO SAYS THAT DRUMMING CAUSES BRAIN DAMAGE.

AND WHAT CAUSED HIS BRAIN DAMAGE?
WHOSE?
STEFANO'S.

'CAUSE HE'S KIND OF STRANGE, TOO.

WHO ISN'T?
IF WE WERE NORMAL, WE WOULDN'T SPEND EVERY DAY IN THE GARAGE WITH 3000 WATTS BLARING AWAY IN OUR EARS.

BOOOOOOMMM
I DON'T KNOW, ALBERTO SEEMS ALL RIGHT TO ME.
YEAH, HE'S ALL RIGHT, BUT STATISTICALLY SPEAKING HE'S LESS NORMAL THAN ANY OF US.

ALL RIGHT. THAT'S ENOUGH.
WHERE ARE YOU OFF TO?

I'M GOING SWIMMING.
NOW?

BUT IT'S ROUGH OUT THERE
AND IT'S FREEZING COLD

AND THERE ARE PEOPLE
AND I'M TOO SKINNY.

I WEIGH 130 POUNDS.
THEY'LL SEE ME. I CAN'T GO OUT THERE.

COME INTO THE WATER, SILLY!
NOBODY'S WATCHING YOU.

OH COME ON GIULIANO!

SEE, NOBODY´S WATCHING YOU!

AAH!

UGH
I´M THE ONLY ONE WHO NOTICES THAT YOU´RE EVEN ALIVE!

OK THEN.

I'M TOTALLY GONNA GET SICK
WITH THIS COLD WEATHER AND ALL. BUT I'LL COME IN ANYWAY!

WATCH OUT, THERE ARE PEOPLE!
THEY'RE WATCHING YOU!

YOU'RE CRAZY!

NOW YOU'RE GONNA GET IT!
HEE HEE HEE

EXPLOITED

STEFANO, IS THAT YOU?

YOU SCARED ME.

I THOUGHT YOU WERE A BURGLAR.

YOU AND DAD SEE BURGLARS EVERYWHERE.
ISN'T HE HERE?

HE'S IN THE DINING ROOM.
WE'RE ABOUT TO HAVE DINNER.

I JUST MET SOMEBODY TODAY. IN THE MUSIC BUSINESS.
CLINK.
HE'S A NEW CLIENT.

HE ORDERED SOME STATUES FROM ME FOR HIS GARDEN.
LUXURY COLLECTION.
VERY EXPENSIVE.
CLINK
CLINK

SCRAPE

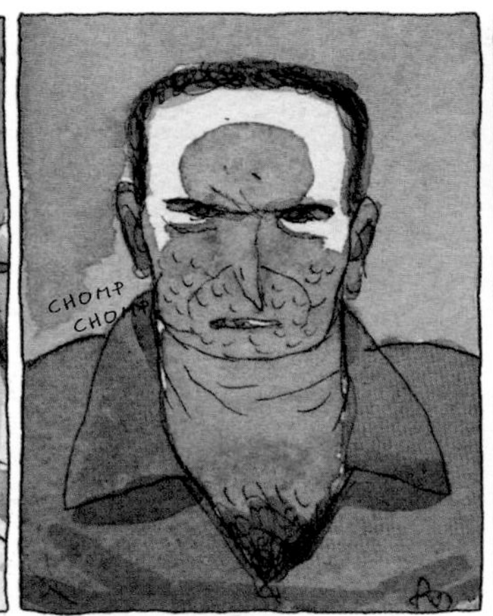
CHOMP
CHOMP

CLINK

THIS GUY I MET WORKS FOR A BIG RECORD COMPANY.

CLINK

HE CAME TO ME FOR A BIG ORDER: A LIFE-SIZE MODEL OF MICHELANGELO'S DAVID.
BLUE ALABASTER. VERY EXPENSIVE.

SO I SAY: "I HAVE A BOY WHO'S HALF-WAY TO BECOMING A MUSICIAN. HE HAS HIS HEART SET ON IT. HE'S OBSESSED."

"IF YOU GIVE HIM A CHANCE, IF YOU LISTEN TO HIM FOR ME, I'LL GIVE YOU AN 18% DISCOUNT. NO ONE COULD DO BETTER THAN THAT."

CLINK

CLACKT
WOULD YOU LIKE ANY MORE MEATBALLS?

NO
I´VE STILL GOT ONE LEFT.

CLINK

ANYWAY

HE'S WILLING TO MEET YOU.
HE LEFT ME HIS BUSINESS CARD.

SHRRF

DO WHAT YOU LIKE WITH IT.

COME AND HAVE DINNER, RENATO.
SO WHAT SHOULD I DO?
I DON'T KNOW.

IT'S GOING TO RAIN.
EVERYTHING I BELIEVED IN HAS DISAPPEARED.
YOU NEED TO THINK ABOUT CLARA.

SHE'S ALL THAT MATTERS NOW.
NOT FOR ME. NOT ANY MORE.
COME AND SIT DOWN. DON'T THINK ABOUT IT.
SCRAPE

SCRA
SINCE DAVID RAN OFF I FEEL DIFFERENT ABOUT THINGS.

MY LOVE FOR CLARA IS A THING OF THE PAST.

GIVE ME YOUR PLATE, ALBERTO.
HOW CAN YOU SAY THAT? HOW CAN YOU CALL THAT LOVE?

IT WAS LOVE, AND ALL LOVE MUST COME TO AN END.
NOT FOR ME.
WHAT DO YOU MEAN?

MAYBE THIS WILL HELP YOU TO UNDERSTAND.
CLICK
WHAT?
HOW'D A GUN GET IN HERE?

WE COULD BUILD A RETRACTABLE UNDERCARRIAGE FOR THE PLANE.
IT'S NOT DIFFICULT. IT'S EASY.
WHAT DO THINK YOU'RE DOING?

BAM!
A RETRACTABLE UNDERCAR-RIAGE?

ALESSANDRO, DEAR, WE'RE SORRY WE GOT ANGRY...

YOUR AUNT AND I WANTED TO APOLOGIZE...

WE DIDN'T REALIZE THAT HE ONLY HAPPENED TO BE THERE...
CAN YOU FORGIVE US?

I'LL FORGIVE YOU ONLY 'CAUSE I'M HUNGRY.
COME AND EAT THEN, DEAR.
AND TOMORROW WE'LL GO TO THE MEMORIAL CHAPEL WITH SOME FLOWERS FOR GRANDDAD'S GRAVE.

YOU'LL COME, WON'T YOU?

OF COURSE I'LL COME. I'VE ALWAYS COME, HAVEN'T I?

ALEX'S BEDROOM WINDOW LOOKS OUT OVER THE CHEMICAL FACTORY YARD.
HIS FATHER WAS A MANAGER AT THE FACTORY FOR YEARS.
ARE WE DOING MINE NOW?
IF WE'RE GONNA DO MINE, I'M TAKING MY SHIRT OFF.
I DID MEET HIM ONCE. HE WAS YOUNG AND REALLY NICE.
AFTER HE DISAPPEARED, THEY DISCOVERED THAT HE'D BEEN EMBEZZLING MONEY FROM THE COMPANY'S ACCOUNTS FOR YEARS, USING A TAX TRICK.
NOBODY'S SEEN HIM SINCE.

THEY SAY HE'S HIDDEN AWAY ON SOME CARIBBEAN ISLAND.

APPARENTLY HE WAS CRAZY ABOUT UNDERWATER FISHING.

THE SONGS THAT ALEX WRITES ARE OFTEN ABOUT THAT.

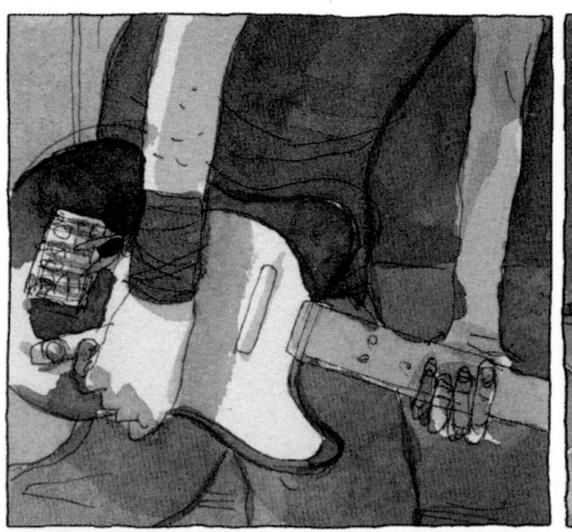

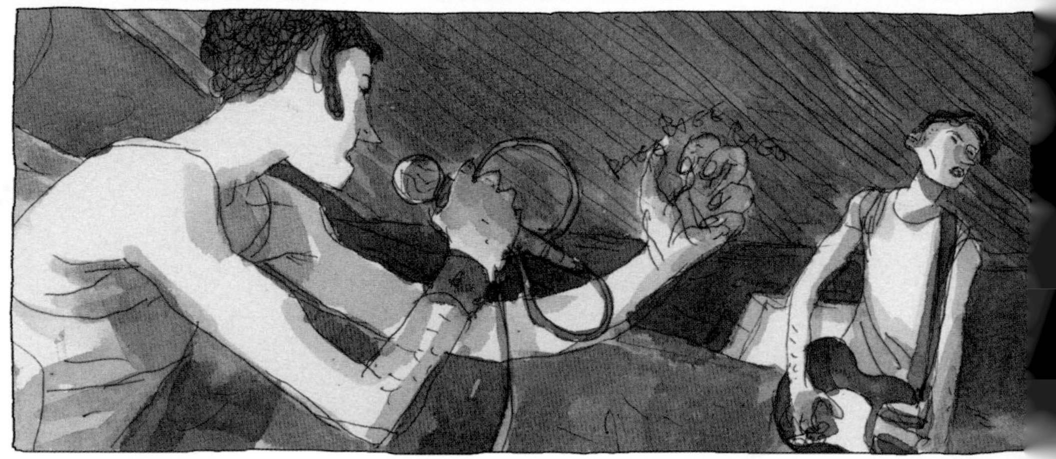

Terza Canzone

NINA!
NINA, YOU'VE GOTTA SEE THIS!

ALEX IS SMOKING!
THIS IS WILD!

SMOKING? SINCE WHEN?

WOW, THAT IS WILD!
HE **IS** SMOKING!

IT'S NOT SMOKE, YOU RETARDS, IT'S STEAM.
IT'S SCIENTIFIC PROOF THAT I WORK HARDER THAN ANYONE ELSE IN HERE.

SO NINA, HAVE YOU COME TO FEEL THE VIBRATORY EFFECT THAT SOUND WAVES HAVE ON FEMALE GENITALIA?

SO THAT'S WHAT HAPPENS?

OH YES, APPARENTLY SO.

OK, GREAT.

OH, NINA
DID GIULIANO TELL YOU WE'VE FOUND A MANAGER?

WE HAVEN'T FOUND A MANAGER.
STOP EXAGGERATING ALL THE TIME.
OF COURSE HE TOLD ME.

THIS A&R MAN WANTS TO HEAR SOME OF OUR SONGS.
I MET HIM, AND I THINK I MADE A REALLY GOOD IMPRESSION.

THAT'S GOOD, ISN'T IT?

YES, IT'S "GOOD" IF WE DON'T MISS THE OPPORTUNITY.
IF WE PRACTICE EVERY DAY AND DON'T THINK ABOUT ANYTHING ELSE.
IF WE CLOSE THE GARAGE DOORS AND LEAVE EVERYTHING ELSE OUTSIDE.

ALBERTO
EXCUSE ME BUT...
WHAT TIME DO YOU HAVE TO GO TODAY?
SOON. BEFORE FIVE.
SEE?
I HAVE TO GO AND HELP MY DAD.
YOU'LL NEVER GET INTO HEAVEN THAT WAY.
RIGHT, LET'S PLAY. LET'S CRANK IT UP.
LET'S MAKE THIS GIRL FEEL THE VIBRATION IN THE FEW MINUTES WE HAVE LEFT.

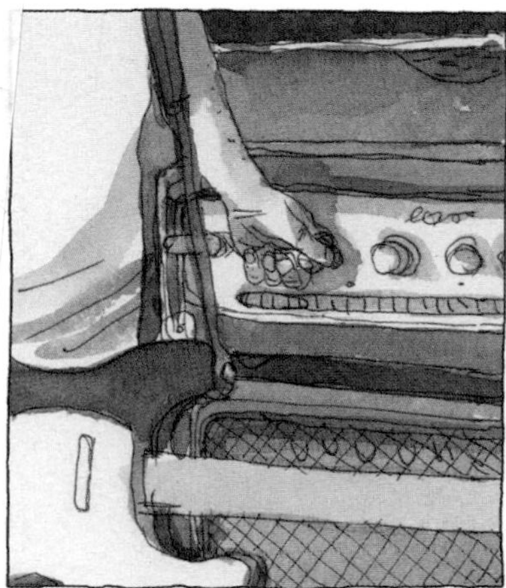

BRAAOOOW
DUN DUM DUN DUM

DUN DUM DUN DUM
PFFF

PFFF?
PFFF PFFF
PLING

PLING PLING PLING
PFFFFF

WOW
THAT'S GOOD.

SO?
WHAT'S YOUR DAD SAY?

BAD NEWS.

HE SAYS THE HEAD'S GONE.
TWO VALVES BURNT OUT. AN OLD MODEL.
YOU CAN'T GET THEM ANY MORE.

FINE, WE'RE SCREWED.
BYE-BYE MANAGER.
MAYBE I CAN THINK OF SOMETHING.

THERE'S NOTHING YOU CAN DO.
YOU NEVER KNOW.
ONE OF GENERAL NOBILE'S OFFICERS MADE A FUSE OUT OF A PENCIL WHEN THEY WERE LOST AT THE NORTH POLE.

YOU CAN STICK YOUR PENCIL UP YOUR ASS, ALBERTO! CAN'T YOU EVER BE SERIOUS FOR JUST A MINUTE?
I AM SERIOUS.

YEAH?
THEN SO AM I.

SERIOUSLY: WHEN I LOOK AT YOU, I SEE FAILURE.
YOU WERE A MUSICIAN. AN A&R MAN WAS EVEN GONNA LISTEN TO YOUR MUSIC.

BUT YOU MISSED YOUR CHANCE.

NOW IT'S TEN YEARS LATER.
I SEE YOUR FUTURE RIGHT NOW. YOU'RE A LOW-RANKING OFFICE WORKER WHO SHARES HIS LIFE WITH A PHOTOCOPIER.

CARE-FUL...
I'VE HEARD THAT PHOTOCOPIER INK MAKES YOU IMPOTENT WITHIN A MONTH.

SO YOU WANNA BE THE JOKER NOW, ALEX?
THE GUY WHO WAS GONNA BE A FAMOUS DRUMMER.
I CAN SEE YOU RIGHT NOW: YOU'RE A HOUSE PAINTER, SPENDING ALL DAY CARRYING A COUPLE OF BUCKETS AROUND.

THERE'S NOTHING WRONG WITH BEING A PAINTER.
ADOLF HITLER WAS A PAINTER AND LOOK WHAT HE BECAME.

LET'S KILL HIM.
ALBERTO
MAYBE IT WOULD BE BETTER IF YOU AND ALEX SWAPPED FUTURES.

I DON'T WANT HIM TO GO FROM PAINTING TO CRAVING WORLD DOMINATION.
HA HA, VERY FUNNY.
CRACK
MEANWHILE, I KNOW WHERE WE CAN GET A NEW AMP.

WHERE?
I'LL TELL YOU IF YOU APOLOGIZE TO THE FÜHRER.

SPEAK UP, ALEX!
OR I'LL KILL YOU.

GRRR
OK, OK, I'LL TELL YOU!
DON'T HURT MY DRUMMING ARM!

EVERY SUNDAY, I GO WITH MY MOM AND MY AUNT TO THE MEMO-RIAL CHAPEL FOR THE SOLDIERS WHO DIED IN THE WAR IN AFRICA.
NEXT TO THE MAIN BUILDING THERE'S A SMALL CONCRETE HOUSE.

IT HAS A WINDOW AT STREET LEVEL. YOU CAN SEE RIGHT IN.

ONE DAY WHEN I WAS GOING BY, I LOOKED IN AND SAW THE INSTRUMENTS.

SCREEE
QUIET!

SH!
CLATTER
CRASH

CLATTER
I THINK THIS MUST BE THE PRACTICE ROOM FOR THE CHURCH GROUP, OR SOMETHING LIKE THAT.

GUYS
THERE'S A TON OF STUFF IN HERE.
THE WAY I SEE IT, THEIR RIGHT TO OWN MUSICAL INSTRUMENTS IS ZILCH.

COME ON, OPEN THE DOOR.
YOU ALL KEEP A LOOKOUT IN CASE ANYBODY COMES.

HEY, THERE'S A CAR COMING!

LET'S HIDE.

LET'S GO!
ALBERTO, THERE'S A CAR COMING.
I'LL SHUT YOU IN. STAY WHERE YOU ARE AND KEEP QUIET UNTIL FURTHER ORDERS.
CLUNK

COME ON GIULIANO!
BRRRRMMM

WHAT'S GOING ON?
I THINK THEY'VE SEEN HIM
BRRRMM

PSSST! GIULIANO!
SCRATCH
BRRRMMMM

GOOD EVENING.

OH NO.
WE'RE SCREWED.
IT'S A MILITARY POLICE CAR.

WHAT ARE YOU DOING IN THE DARK, NINA?

NOTHING.

WHAT DO YOU MEAN, NOTHING?
CLICK

NO, LEAVE IT OFF.
I'VE GOT A HEADACHE.
CLICK

HOW COME?
I DON'T KNOW.

AREN'T YOU SEEING GIULIANO THIS EVENING?
NO.

HE'S OUT. HE HAD TO DO SOMETHING WITH HIS DAD.

WHAT'S HE LIKE?
HIS FATHER? HE BREEDS HUNTING DOGS. HE'S OBSESSED WITH THEM.

DOGS ARE LOVELY.
YEAH. THEY'RE ALL RIGHT.
BUT HE'S REALLY OBSESSED.

BRRRRMMM

COME HERE.
I'LL SHOW YOU SOMETHING

WHAT?

GIULIANO TOLD ME THAT WHEN HE WAS A KID, HIS FATHER NEVER TOOK A PICTURE OF HIM. NOT ONCE.

HE ONLY TOOK PICTURES OF THE DOGS.

ONE DAY HIS MOM GOT ANGRY. SHE WAS FED UP WITH ALL THESE DOG PICTURES.
THERE WASN'T A SINGLE PHOTOGRAPH OF HER OWN CHILD IN THE WHOLE HOUSE.

SO WHAT HAPPENED?
SO HIS DAD STARTED STANDING HIM NEXT TO THE DOGS HE WAS PHOTOGRAPHING.

AND NOW THERE ARE NO PHOTOS OF GIULIANO AS A KID WITHOUT A DOG NEXT TO HIM.

LOOK, ISN'T HE GORGEOUS?

YES.
WHAT BREED IS HE?

HEE HEE HEE!
I'M GONNA KILL YOU!
STOP! YOU'LL MAKE ME SPILL MY COFFEE!

HEE HEE HEE! STOP, STOP! HEE HEE!
HEE HEE HEE!

WHAT NOW? ARE YOU TRYING TO TELL ME YOU DON'T KNOW THIS IS A MILITARY ZONE?
NO UNAUTHORIZED ACCESS.
I THOUGHT THE MILITARY ZONE ONLY INCLUDED THE AIRPORT.
OH, REALLY?
ZONA MILITARE
YES. I COME HERE A LOT.
I KNOW THE AREA, BECAUSE MY GRANDDAD IS BURIED IN THE MEMORIAL CHAPEL.
HE WAS KILLED IN AFRICA. IN THE WAR.
HIS GRANDDAD?
BUT IT WAS MY GRANDDAD WHO DIED IN THE WAR!
BE QUIET, YOU JERK! WHAT DOES IT MATTER?

WAS HE A SOLDIER?
YES, SIR.

IN THE AIR FORCE
LIKE YOU.
I WAS BROUGHT UP TO REMEMBER HIS HEROISM.

GOD, COUNTRY, AND FAMILY. REAL VALUES.

HE'S TAKEN THE WORDS OUT OF MY MOUTH!
SEMPER FIDELIS
SEMPER

PFFF

D-DM D-DM

I MUST BE THE GREATEST ACTOR ALIVE.
BRRRRMMM

YES!
HEY GUYS, HELP ME!

HELP ME, GUYS!

BE CAREFUL NOT TO BREAK IT. IT'S BRAND NEW.
I'LL BE RIGHT THERE.

LET'S GO, ALBERTO, WHAT ARE YOU DOING?

HEY, ALBERTO, COME ON! I CAN HEAR SOMETHING!

LET'S GO!
BONK

WHERE DID YOU FIND THAT BASS?
CLIIP

ALBERTO!
DID YOU SEE IF THERE WAS A GUITAR FOR ME TOO?

WHA?

HE WHO DARES, WINS.
CLICK

WHERE THERE'S A WILL, THERE'S A WAY.

I'VE HEARD THOSE WORDS SO MANY TIMES.

BUT ONLY NOW DO I REALIZE THEIR TRUE MEANING.

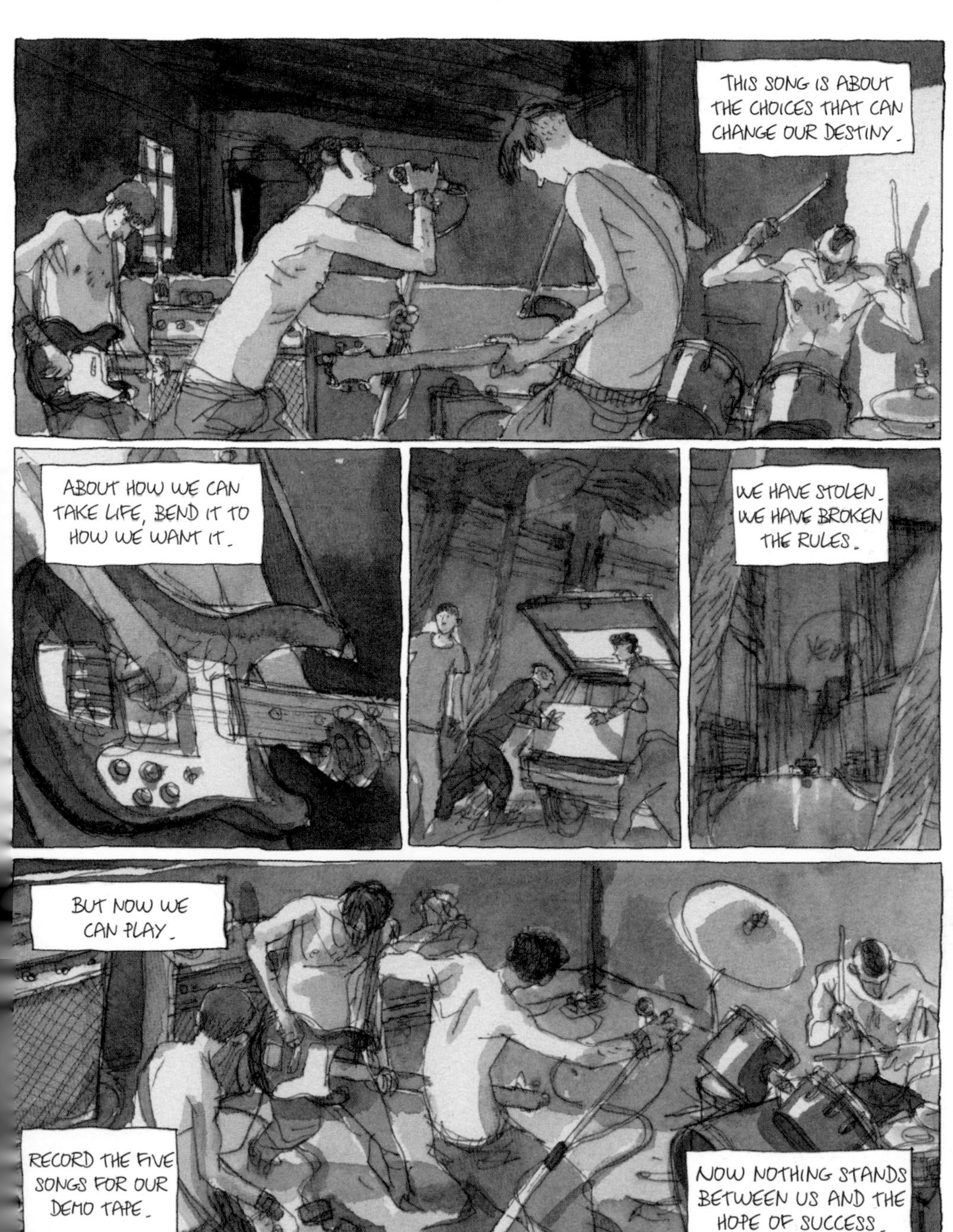
THIS SONG IS ABOUT THE CHOICES THAT CAN CHANGE OUR DESTINY.
ABOUT HOW WE CAN TAKE LIFE, BEND IT TO HOW WE WANT IT.
WE HAVE STOLEN. WE HAVE BROKEN THE RULES.
BUT NOW WE CAN PLAY.
RECORD THE FIVE SONGS FOR OUR DEMO TAPE.
NOW NOTHING STANDS BETWEEN US AND THE HOPE OF SUCCESS.

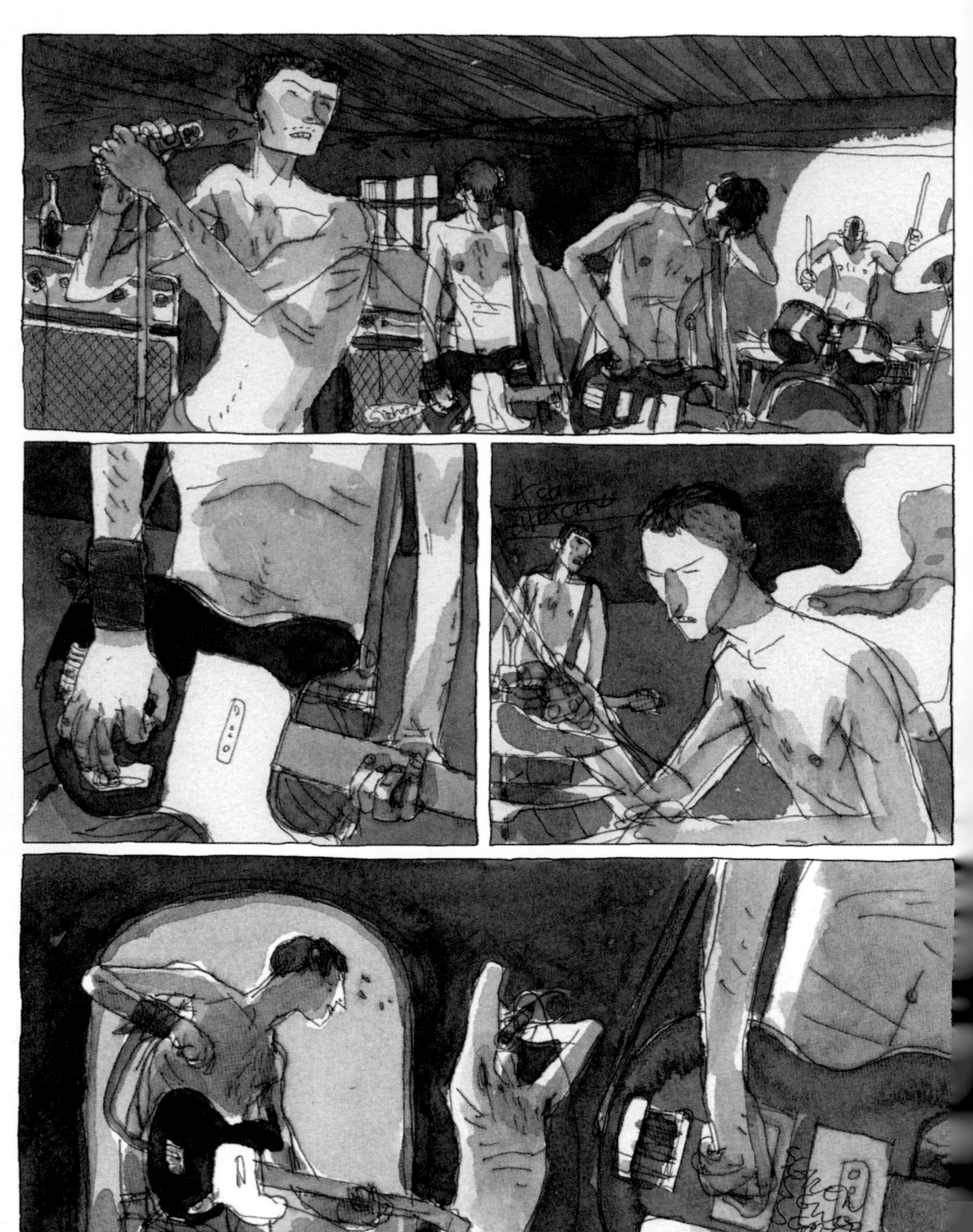

Quarta Canzone

I'M AN IDIOT.
A LIAR. A FOOL.

IN SHORT, I'VE SCREWED UP BIG TIME.
BUT I WASN'T REALLY WITH IT. I WASN'T THINKING STRAIGHT.

ALBERTO HAD FOUND THIS AWESOME BASS.

BUT MY GUITAR'S OK, ISN'T IT?

I DON'T NEED ANOTHER ONE.
YOUR GUITAR IS CRAP - SO IT'S PERFECT FOR YOU.

HA HA HA
ON THE WAY HOME WE WERE JOKING AROUND.

GO ON, LAUGH IF YOU WANT TO.
AFTER ALL, YOU FASCISTS ARE ALL FAGGOTS.

YOU FILTHY RED SKULL!
ARGH... HA HA
WE THOUGHT WE'D OUTSMARTED THE WORLD.

WE'VE DONE IT, GUYS! THE WORLD IS OURS!

VROOM

THE DAY AFTER, WE PLAYED REALLY WELL.
WITH MORE POWER THAN EVER BEFORE.

IT WAS ONLY AFTER THE PRACTICE THAT I REMEMBERED THE WALLET.
IS THAT A NEW FASHION OR DID YOU RIP YOUR POCKET?
IT HAD ALL MY DOCUMENTS IN IT, WITH MY NAME AND ADDRESS.
AND NOW I'M AFRAID I LOST IT NEAR THE MEMORIAL CHAPEL.
I'M DATING AN IDIOT.
ONE WHO GOES OUT STEALING.
BUT I ONLY DID IT FOR STEFANO!
DO YOU KNOW HIS BROTHER DIED OF SOME STRANGE DISEASE?
I KNOW. IT'S A SHAME. BUT HOW IS THAT RELEVANT?

IT IS RELEVANT. I'VE SEEN HIM MISERABLE FOR SO LONG.
UNTIL WE STARTED PLAYING AGAIN IN THE GARAGE.

HE'S STILL OBSESSED WITH DEATH AND FATAL ILLNESSES.
BUT NOW HE HAS MUSIC TOO.

AND THIS THING WITH THE A&R MAN FINALLY GOT HIM THINKING ABOUT SOMETHING ELSE.

IF WE'D STOPPED...
IF WE'D HAD TO STOP PLAYING, HE'D HAVE TAKEN IT REALLY BADLY.

AND I DIDN'T WANT HIM TO GET MISERABLE AGAIN.

CLICK

SWDOO8H

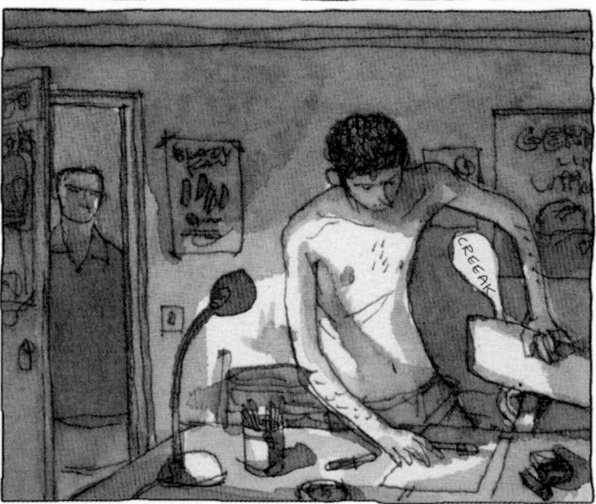
CREEAK

EVERYTHING'S FINE, DAD.
I JUST WENT TO THE BATHROOM.

STEFANO SAYS HE'LL WRITE A SONG FOR HIS BROTHER ONE DAY.

BUT HE'LL ONLY DO IT WHEN HE'S SURE HE WON'T WRITE ANYTHING TOO CHEESY.
UNTIL THEN, HE SAYS, HE WON'T WRITE A LINE OR SING A SINGLE WORD.

WHEEEEEE
SO WHAT DID YOU DO ABOUT THE AMP?
SNIFF
I FIXED IT.
GOOD JOB.
IT WASN'T EASY.
WATCH THIS.
CLICK
WHEEEEEE
BZZZZ
SNIFF
CLUNK
PERFECT.
WHAT ABOUT THE BURNT-OUT VALVES?
DON'T TELL ME YOU FIXED THOSE?
YEP.

SO THERE YOU GO.
THE BIGGEST LIE OF ALL.

THIS IS WHERE I'M REUNITED WITH THE WALLET
IN THE GARAGE
AND WITH THE WALLET IS MY FATHER.
ALONG WITH FOUR LONG-HAIRED METAL-HEADS.
AND OUR AMP.
ALBERTO'S NEW BASS.

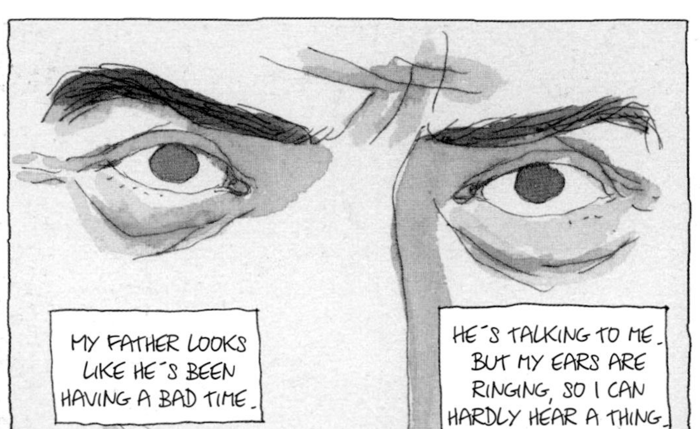
MY FATHER LOOKS LIKE HE'S BEEN HAVING A BAD TIME.
HE'S TALKING TO ME. BUT MY EARS ARE RINGING, SO I CAN HARDLY HEAR A THING.

BZZZZZZZZZZZZZZZ

I SEE HIM SIGNING A CHECK.
I GET THE IMPRESSION HE HAS A BLACK EYE.

RRRRIP
BUT IT COULD JUST BE A SHADOW.

WHO ARE THESE MEN?

THESE MEN ARE THE "FALLEN ANGELS."
THE THINGS YOU STOLE BELONG TO THEM.

I WANT YOU TO THANK THEM FOR NOT PRESSING CHARGES.

NO. THANK THEM PROPERLY.
BECAUSE THEY WERE PERCEPTIVE ENOUGH TO SEE THAT YOU'RE JUST SOME KIDS WHO DON'T KNOW ANY BETTER.
SO THEY SPARED YOU HAVING TO GO TO PRISON.

THANK YOU
THANK YOU

SO WHAT KIND OF MUSIC DO YOU PLAY?

DEATH METAL, HOW ABOUT YOU?
LET'S GO!
COME ON!

COME HERE, YOU GUYS.

THE GARAGE NEEDS TO BE EMPTY BY TOMORROW.
EVERY-THING GOES.

TAKE YOUR STUFF AND GET RID OF IT.
SUPPOSING THAT IT'S REALLY "YOUR STUFF."
YEAH, THE DRUM KIT'S MINE!
I BOUGHT IT MYSELF WITH MY OWN MONEY.

OH YEAH? AND WHAT'S YOUR JOB?
WHAT DO YOU EARN?

BOM

FORGET IT.

BE THAT AS IT MAY, THESE AREN'T MY THINGS. THE GARAGE, ON THE OTHER HAND, IS.
ANYTHING LEFT IN HERE TOMORROW EVENING WILL BE PUT OUT IN THE STREET.

YOU KNEW THE RULE ABOUT USING THE PLACE, DIDN'T YOU?
OF COURSE WE DID.
CLICK

THEN THERE'S NO MORE TO BE SAID.

WOOF
WOOF
WOOF
WOOF
WOOF

Quinta Canzone

THE TRUTH IS THAT ALL MEN ARE CANNIBALS BY NATURE.
I UNDER-STAND.

AT LEAST, I THINK I UNDERSTAND.

THERE ARE ONLY THREE SONGS ON THE TAPE BECAUSE EVERYTHING WENT WRONG...
AND THEY MIGHT NOT BE RECORDED VERY WELL BECAUSE WE ONLY HAD ONE...
STOP
HANG ON A MINUTE, AMIGO.

YOU HAVEN'T UNDERSTOOD AT ALL, OR ELSE YOU WEREN'T LISTENING.
THIS TAPE COULD CONTAIN THE MOST BEAUTIFUL MUSIC IN THE WORLD. "THE NEW BEATLES." IT WOULDN'T MAKE ANY DIFFERENCE.

THE MARKET IS ALL THAT MATTERS. THE MUSIC ISN'T IMPORTANT.

I'LL SAY IT ONE MORE TIME: THE RECORD COMPANY HAS DECIDED NOT TO MAKE ANY MORE INVESTMENTS IN NEW ARTISTS.
IT'S A STRATEGY, LIKE ANY OTHER.

BUT LISTEN: I OWE A DEBT TO YOUR FATHER.
I TOLD HIM I'D HELP YOU AND I ALWAYS KEEP MY WORD.

SWOOSH

NOW COME OUT ONTO THE TERRACE.
I'LL SHOW YOU SOMETHING.
SCRATCH

THE ACTOR BEN AFFLECK HAS ONE JUST LIKE IT IN HIS LOS ANGELES VILLA.

IT'S EMPTY.
IT'S A SWIMMING POOL.

SO?
DO YOU LIKE IT?
WHY IS IT EMPTY?

LISTEN CAREFULLY. THIS IS MY SUGGESTION: I CAN GIVE YOU A JOB AT OUR HEAD OFFICE.

I KNOW IT'S NOT A RECORD DEAL, BUT YOU'LL BE IN REGULAR CONTACT WITH REAL MUSICIANS - STARS.
YOU HAVE A CERTAIN CHARISMA.
THERE'LL BE THOUSANDS OF OPPORTUNITIES TO GET YOURSELF NOTICED.

AND WHAT DO I TELL THE OTHERS?
DON'T TELL THEM ANYTHING.
WHAT SHOULD YOU TELL THEM? IT'S YOUR LIFE.
YOU DON'T WANT TO STAY HERE IN THE STICKS, JAMMING WITH A BUNCH OF JERKS.
LOSERS WITHOUT A FUTURE.
BUT YOU DON'T KNOW THEM. THEY PLAY WELL.
YOU CAN HEAR IT ON THE TAPE...
ARE YOU STILL GOING ON ABOUT THAT DAMNED TAPE?
I'LL TELL YOU AGAIN FOR THE LAST TIME. THE MUSIC IS NOT IMPORTANT. IT'S THE DESIRE FOR SUCCESS THAT COUNTS.
THE WILL TO TAKE ON THE WORLD.
DO YOU HAVE THE WILL TO DO THAT?

I MEAN...
DO YOU **REALLY** HAVE IT?

BZZZZZZZZZZZ
BRRRRHAM
BRRRRMMM

RRRRMMM

OOF...
I KNOW YOU'RE STILL WONDERING ABOUT THAT QUESTION.
FINE. ASK AWAY - I'LL ANSWER.

GO ON - ASK.

WHY IS YOUR FACE BLUE?

NOT THAT QUESTION!
ASK ME THE REAL ONE.

HOW DID I BUY THE DRUMS?
HOW HAVE I MANAGED TO LIVE ALL THIS TIME WITHOUT EVER WORKING?

HMMM
SUPPORTED BY YOUR MOM AND YOUR AUNT, MAYBE?

COULD BE.
ACTUALLY, NO. THEY DON'T WORK EITHER.
THEY SPEND ALL DAY IN THE HOUSE BITCHING ABOUT PEOPLE.
THEY ONLY HAVE THEIR PENSIONS.

SO?
EVERY MONTH, FOR YEARS, ALEX HAS RECEIVED MONEY FROM A BANK IN TRINIDAD.
MONEY FROM THE CARIBBEAN.

HIS FATHER SENT HIM THE MONEY UNTIL HE REACHED EIGHTEEN.
SCRATCH
SECRET MONEY THAT CAME WITHOUT A SINGLE WORD.
THE MONEY - THAT WAS ALL.

ALEX SAYS HE NEVER USED THIS MONEY, ON PRINCIPLE.
ACNE CREAM? BUT YOU'VE NEVER HAD A ZIT IN YOUR LIFE.
THAT'S BECAUSE IT'S SUCH A GOOD CREAM.
WELL, ALMOST NEVER.

EXCEPT FOR THE MOST IMPORTANT THINGS: THE DRUMS, THE MOPED, CONCERTS, RECORDS, CIGARETTES, BEER, CLOTHES...
BZZZZZZZZZ

AND THIS TIME I USED IT FOR THIS. SO NOW IT'S GONE AND I DON'T HAVE TO THINK ABOUT IT ANY MORE.
BUT IT'S HUGE!
IT BELONGED TO A FORMER EMPLOYEE OF MY DAD. A SHARP GUY.

HE LEFT THE FACTORY AND SET UP ON HIS OWN.
HE ALSO TOLD ME A BUNCH OF ARGUMENTS IN FAVOR OF COMMUNISM.

THEY WERE PRETTY SMART IN RUSSIA IN THE SIXTIES.
DID YOU KNOW THAT?

THE NEXT SONG WILL BE ABOUT HOW WE LOST THE GARAGE.
IT'LL BE THE STORY OF THE THEFT FROM THE MEMORIAL CHAPEL
AND WILL TELL ABOUT ALEX'S TREASURE.
IT WILL BE ABOUT OUR PARENTS AND MY FATHER'S OBSESSION WITH DOGS.
AND ABOUT HOW THINGS COME TO AN END.
AND BEGIN AGAIN.

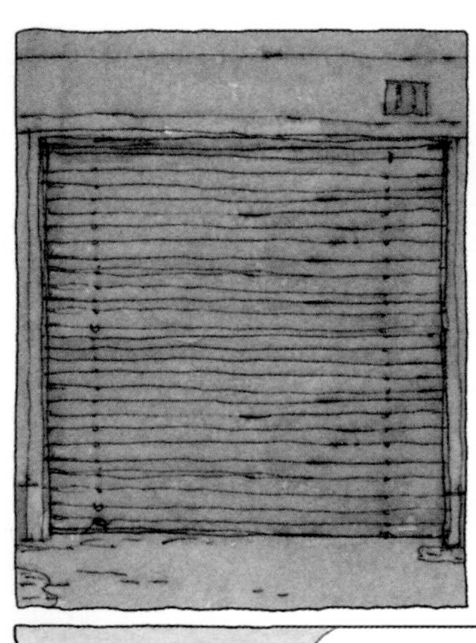

THIS IS IT.

THIS IS THE PLACE.
WOW!
SLAP
SLAP
SLAP
A SHEET METAL HANGAR.
WE'LL GET HEATSTROKE - MENINGITIS IS INEVITABLE.

YOU THINK?
SCRATCH
DON'T LISTEN TO HIM, THIS PLACE IS GREAT!

Garage Band

Studies

1
2
SBRANO
5

E NOI
SHE
10 10 10

UNA VIÀ
È TUO!

ANXIETY

GIULIANO
ALBERTO
STEFANO
NO! OCCHI IN SU!
ALEX DETTO
GIULIANO
GLI OCCHI!!
NUOVO MODELLO

IO LAVORO PER SONY ENTERPRISE

ME?
TCHA
TCHA

New York & London

Published by First Second
First Second is an imprint of Roaring Brook Press, a division of Holtzbrinck Publishing Holdings Limited Partnership
175 Fifth Avenue, New York, NY 10010

Distributed in Canada by H. B. Fenn and Company Ltd.
Distributed in the United Kingdom by Macmillan Children's Books, a division of Pan Macmillan.

Originally published in France in 2005 under the title *Le Local* by Gallimard Jeunesse, Paris.

Design by Danica Novgorodoff.

Library of Congress Cataloging-in-Publication Data

Gipi, 1963- .
[Local. English]
Garage band / Gipi. -- 1st American ed.
p. cm.
ISBN-13: 978-1-59643-206-2
ISBN-10: 1-59643-206-3

1. Graphic novels. I. Title.
PN6767.G56L6313 2007
741.5'945--dc22

2006018345

First Second books are available for special promotions and premiums.
For details, contact: Director of Special Markets, Holtzbrinck Publishers.

First American Edition April 2007

Printed in China

10 9 8 7 6 5 4 3 2